The Reluctant Dragon

Based on the story by
Kenneth Grahame

Retold by Katie Daynes

Illustrated by Fred Blunt

One evening,
long ago, a shepherd
ran home, terrified.

2

"It has long, sharp claws...

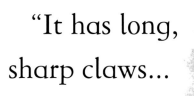

a long, pointy tail...

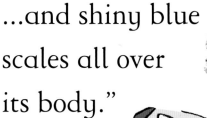

...and shiny blue scales all over its body."

His son looked up
from his book.

"That sounds like a
dragon," he said.

"A dragon?" yelped the wife.

"A *dragon*?" said the shepherd.

"That does not sound good."

The boy wasn't
scared. The next day,
he set off up the hill
to find the
dragon.

Bye. Don't
worry!

"He might be friendly," thought the boy.

The dragon *was* friendly – and he was thrilled to see the boy.

It's beautiful here, but it does get lonely.

The boy smiled. He sat
down and asked the dragon
all kinds of questions.

The dragon told stories of long, long ago.

There were dangerous dragons everywhere.

And brave knights fought them to rescue princesses.

The boy came back every day to hear the stories.

But then the villagers found out about the dragon. They were terrified.

SLAY THE DRAGON

BAN THE DRAGON

BANISH THE DRAGON

SLAY THE DRAGON

BANISH THE DRAGON

SLAY THE DRAGON

The boy ran straight to the
dragon. "The villagers want
to get rid of you!" he panted.

That afternoon, the boy heard even worse news.

"Saint George the Dragon Killer wants to fight you," gasped the boy.

"I'll just hide in my cave
until he goes away," said
the dragon.

"You can't!" cried the boy.
"Everyone wants a fight!"

The dragon yawned.
"I'm sure you'll think of
something," he said.

The boy walked slowly
back down to the village.

"It's not true!" said the boy.
"The dragon wouldn't hurt
a fly."

"But everyone wants a fight," said George. "What can I do?"

"Follow me," said the boy. And he took George to meet the dragon.

25

"What a perfect place for a fight," said George.

"No fighting," said the dragon, firmly.

"Not even a
pretend fight?"
asked the boy.

"Maybe…"
said the dragon.

27

The boy turned to George.
"Do you promise not to
hurt him?"

"Well, it has to look
real," said George.

"Will there be a feast
afterwards?" asked
the dragon.

"There will, and you can
come," promised George.

29

The next morning,
lots of villagers
arrived to watch
the fight.

The boy waited nervously by the dragon's cave.

They cheered and waved when Saint George rode into view. But where was the dragon?

32

Then a roar echoed around
the hills. Flames filled
the air.

Everyone gasped as the dragon appeared. His scales sparkled and he breathed out fire.

"Charge!" cried George.
He galloped hard, his spear
held high.

The dragon bounded up.

And they shot past each other.

"Missed!" yelled the crowd.

George and the dragon turned around and charged again.

37

This time, there was no way they could miss.
CLATTER! BANG! OUF!

The dragon slumped to the ground. George towered over him.

Cut off his head!

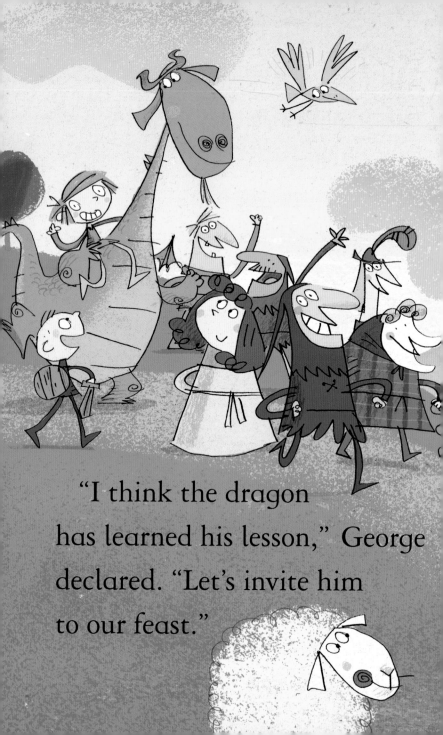

"I think the dragon
has learned his lesson," George
declared. "Let's invite him
to our feast."

And he led the villagers,
the boy and the dragon back
down the hill.

The boy was happy
because his plan worked.

The villagers were
happy because they'd seen
a fight. George was happy
because he'd won.

The dragon was happiest of all. He had lots of new friends...

...and a very full tummy.

"Jolly night it's been," he murmured and began to snore.

"How will I get him
home?" said the boy.

"I'll help," said George.
He gave the dragon a prod.

And they set off up the
hill arm-in-arm – the saint,
the dragon and the boy.

About the story

The Reluctant Dragon was first published over 100 years ago. The author, Kenneth Grahame, also wrote the famous children's story *The Wind in the Willows*.

Designed by Caroline Spatz
Digital manipulation: John Russell
Series editor: Lesley Sims
Series designer: Russell Punter

This edition first published in 2013 by Usborne Publishing Ltd., Usborne House, 83-85 Saffron Hill, London EC1N 8RT, England. www.usborne.com Copyright © 2013, 2009 Usborne Publishing Ltd.